A Sound of Thunder

Ray Bradbury

LOOKING FORWARD

When a group of hunters travels back in time to hunt dinosaurs, one man stumbles off the designated path, killing a butterfly and changing the course of history.

WORDS TO WATCH FOR

Here are some words that may be unfamiliar. Use this list as a guide to better understanding. Examine it before you begin to read.

annihilate—destroy; wipe out
expendable—replaceable; dispensable
infinitesimally—in an immeasurably small way
merest—slightest
paradox—contradiction; inconsistency
resilient—flexible; springy
sheathed—covered; protected
subtle—not obvious; difficult to understand
undulate—rise and fall; ripple
waxes—grows; develops

Text credit: "A Sound of Thunder" by Ray Bradbury. Reprinted by permission of Don Congdon Associates, Inc. Copyright © 1952 by the Crowell–Collier Publishing Co., renewed 1980 by Ray Bradbury.

A Sound of Thunder

by Ray Bradbury

The sign on the wall seemed to quaver under a film of sliding warm water. Eckels felt his eyelids blink over his stare, and the sign burned in this momentary darkness:

TIME SAFARI, INC.
SAFARIS TO ANY YEAR IN THE PAST.
YOU NAME THE ANIMAL.
WE TAKE YOU THERE.
YOU SHOOT IT.

A warm phlegm gathered in Eckels's throat; he swallowed and pushed it down. The muscles around his mouth formed a smile as he put his hand slowly out upon the air, and in that hand waved a check for ten thousand dollars to the man behind the desk.

"Does this safari guarantee I come back alive?"

"We guarantee nothing," said the official, "except the dinosaurs." He turned. "This is Mr. Travis, your Safari Guide in the Past. He'll tell you what and where to shoot. If he says no shooting, no shooting. If you disobey instructions, there's a stiff penalty of another ten thousand dollars, plus possible government action, on your return."

Eckels glanced across the vast office at a mass

and tangle, a snaking and humming of wires and steel boxes, at an aurora that flickered now orange, now silver, now blue. There was a sound like a gigantic bonfire burning all of Time, all the years and all the parchment calendars, all the hours piled high and set aflame.

A touch of the hand and this burning would, on the instant, beautifully reverse itself. Eckels remembered the wording in the advertisements to the letter. Out of chars and ashes, out of dust and coals, like golden salamanders, the old years, the green years, might leap; roses sweeten the air, white hair turn Irish-black, wrinkles vanish; all, everything fly back to seed, flee death, rush down to their beginnings, suns rise in western skies and set in glorious easts, moons eat themselves opposite to the custom, all and everything cupping one in another like Chinese boxes, rabbits into hats, all and everything returning to the fresh death, the seed death, the green death, to the time before the beginning. A touch of a hand might do it, the merest touch of a hand.

"Unbelievable." Eckels breathed, the light of the Machine on his thin face. "A real Time Machine." He shook his head. "Makes you think. If the election had gone badly yesterday, I might be here now running away from the results. Thank God Keith won. He'll make a fine President of the United States."

"Yes," said the man behind the desk. "We're lucky. If Deutscher had gotten in, we'd have the worst kind of dictatorship. There's an anti everything man for you, a militarist, anti-Christ, anti-human, anti-intellectual. People called us up, you know, joking but not joking. Said if Deutscher became President, they wanted to go live in 1942. Of course it's not our business to conduct escapes, but to form safaris. Anyway, Keith's President now. All you got to worry about is—"

"Shooting my dinosaur," Eckels finished it for him.

"A *Tyrannosaurus rex*. The Tyrant Lizard, the most incredible monster in history. Sign this release. Anything happens to you, we're not responsible. Those dinosaurs are hungry."

Eckels flushed angrily. "Trying to scare me!"

"Frankly, yes. We don't want anyone going who'll panic at the first shot. Six safari leaders were killed last year, and a dozen hunters. We're here to give you the severest thrill a real hunter ever asked for. Traveling you back sixty million years to bag the biggest game in all of Time. Your personal check's still there. Tear it up."

Mr. Eckels looked at the check. His fingers twitched.

"Good luck," said the man behind the desk. "Mr. Travis, he's all yours."

They moved silently across the room, taking their guns with them, toward the Machine, toward the silver metal and the roaring light.

* * *

First a day and then a night and then a day and then a night, then it was day-night-day-night-day. A week, a month, a year, a decade! A.D. 2055. A.D. 2019. 1999! 1957! Gone! The Machine roared.

They put on their oxygen helmets and tested the intercoms.

Eckels swayed on the padded seat, his face pale, his jaw stiff. He felt the trembling in his arms, and he looked down and found his hands tight on the new rifle. There were four other men in the Machine. Travis, the Safari Leader; his assistant, Lesperance; and two other hunters, Billings and Kramer. They sat looking at each other, and the years blazed around them.

"Can these guns get a dinosaur cold?" Eckels felt his mouth saying.

"If you hit them right," said Travis on the helmet radio. "Some dinosaurs have two brains, one in the head, another far down the spinal column. We stay away from those. That's stretching luck. Put your first two shots into the eyes, if you can, blind them, and go back into the brain."

The Machine howled. Time was a film run backwards. Suns fled and ten million moons fled after them. "Think," said Eckels. "Every hunter that ever lived would envy us today. This makes Africa seem like Illinois."

The Machine slowed; its scream fell to a murmur. The Machine stopped.

The sun stopped in the sky.

The fog that had enveloped the Machine blew away, and they were in an old time, a very old time indeed, three hunters and two Safari Heads with their blue metal guns across their knees.

"Christ isn't born yet," said Travis. "Moses has not gone to the mountain to talk with God. The Pyramids are still in the earth, waiting to be cut out and put up. *Remember* that. Alexander, Caesar, Napoleon, Hitler—none of them exists."

The man nodded.

"That"—Mr. Travis pointed—"is the jungle of sixty million, two thousand and fifty-five years before President Keith."

He indicated a metal path that struck off into green wilderness, over streaming swamp, among giant ferns and palms.

"And that," he said, "is the Path, laid by Time Safari for your use. It floats six inches above the earth. Doesn't touch so much as one grass blade, flower, or tree. It's an anti-gravity metal. Its purpose is to keep you from touching this world of the past in any way. Stay on the Path. Don't go off it. I repeat, *don't go off.* For *any* reason! If you fall off, there's a penalty. And don't shoot any animal we don't okay."

"Why?" asked Eckels.

They sat in the ancient wilderness. Far birds' cries blew on a wind, and the smell of tar and old salt sea, moist grasses, and flowers the color of blood.

"We don't want to change the Future. We don't belong here in the Past. The government doesn't *like* us here. We have to pay big graft to keep our franchise. A Time Machine is finicky business. Not knowing it, we might kill an important animal, a small bird, a roach, a flower even, thus destroying an important link in a growing species."

"That's not clear," said Eckels.

"All right," Travis continued, "say we accidentally kill one mouse here. That means all the future families of this one particular mouse are destroyed, right?"

"Right."

"And all the families of the families of the families of that one mouse! With a stamp of your foot, you annihilate first one, then a dozen, then a thousand, a million, a *billion* possible mice!"

"So they're dead," said Eckels. "So what?"

"So what?" Travis snorted quietly. "Well, what about the foxes that'll need those mice to survive? For want of ten mice, a fox dies. For want of ten foxes, a lion starves. For want of a lion, all manner of insects, vultures, infinite billions of life forms are thrown into chaos and destruction. Eventually it all boils down to this: fifty-nine million years later, a caveman, one of a dozen on the *entire world*, goes hunting wild boar or saber-toothed tiger for food. But you, friend, have *stepped* on all the tigers in that region. By stepping on *one* single mouse. So the caveman starves. And the caveman, please note, is not just *any* expendable man, no! He is an *entire future nation*. From his loins would have sprung ten sons. From *their* loins one hundred sons, and thus onward to a civilization. Destroy this one man, and you destroy a race, a people, an entire history of life. It is comparable to slaying some of Adam's grandchildren. The stomp of your foot, on one mouse, could start an earthquake, the effects of which could shake our earth and destinies down through Time to their very foundations. With the death of that one caveman, a billion others yet unborn are throttled in the womb. Perhaps Rome never rises on its seven hills. Perhaps Europe is forever a dark forest, and only Asia waxes healthy and teeming. Step on a mouse, and you crush the pyramids. Step on a mouse, and you leave your print, like a Grand Canyon, across Eternity. Queen Elizabeth might never be born, Washington might not cross the Delaware, there might never be a United States at all. So be careful. Stay on the Path. *Never* step off!"

"I see," said Eckels. "Then it wouldn't pay for us even to touch the *grass*?"

"Correct. Crushing certain plants could add up infinitesimally. A little error here could multiply in sixty million years, all out of proportion. Of course, maybe our theory is wrong. Maybe Time *can't* be changed by us. Or maybe it can be changed only in little, subtle ways. A dead mouse here makes an insect imbalance there, a population disproportion later, a bad harvest further on, a depression, mass starvation, and, finally, a change in *social* temperament in far-flung countries. Something much more subtle, like that. Perhaps only a soft breath, a whisper, a hair, pollen on the air, such a slight, slight change that unless you looked close you wouldn't see it. Who knows? Who really can say he knows? We don't know. We're guessing. But until we do know for certain whether our messing around in Time *can* make a big roar or a little rustle in history, we're being careful. This Machine, this Path, your clothing and bodies, were sterilized, as you know, before the journey. We wear these oxygen helmets so we can't introduce our bacteria into an ancient atmosphere."

"How do we know which animals to shoot?"

"They're marked with red paint," said Travis. "Today, before our journey, we sent Lesperance here back with the Machine. He came to this particular era and followed certain animals."

"Studying them?"

"Right," said Lesperance. "I track them through their entire existence, noting which of them lives longest. Very few. How many times they mate. Not often. Life's short. When I find one that's going to die when a tree falls on him, or one that drowns in a tar pit, I note the exact hour, minute, and second. I shoot a paint bomb. It leaves a red patch on his side. We can't miss it. Then I correlate our arrival in the Past so that we meet the monster not more than two minutes before he would have died anyway. This way, we kill only animals with no future, that are never going to mate again. You see how *careful* we are?"

"But if you came back this morning in Time," said Eckels eagerly, "you must've bumped into us, our Safari! How did it turn out? Was it successful? Did all of us get through—alive?"

Travis and Lesperance gave each other a look.

"That'd be a paradox," said the latter. "Time does-n't permit that sort of mess—a man meeting himself. When such occasions threaten, Time steps aside. Like an airplane hitting an air pocket. You felt the Machine jump just before we stopped? That was us passing ourselves on the way back to the Future. We saw nothing. There's no way of telling *if* this expe-dition was a success, *if* we got our monster, or whether all of us—meaning *you*, Mr. Eckels—got out alive."

Eckels smiled palely.

"Cut that," said Travis sharply. "Everyone on his feet!"

They were ready to leave the Machine.

The jungle was high and the jungle was broad and the jungle was the entire world forever and forever. Sounds like music and sounds like flying tents filled the sky, and those were pterodactyls soaring with cavernous gray wings, gigantic bats of delirium and night fever. Eckels, balanced on the narrow Path, aimed his rifle playfully.

"Stop that!" said Travis. "Don't even aim for fun, blast you! If your gun should go off—"

Eckels flushed. "Where's our *Tyrannosaurus*?"

Lesperance checked his wristwatch. "Up ahead. We'll bisect his trail in sixty seconds. Look for the red paint! Don't shoot till we give the word. Stay on the Path. *Stay on the Path*!"

They moved forward in the wind of morning.

"Strange," murmured Eckels. "Up ahead, sixty million years, Election Day over. Keith made President. Everyone celebrating. And here we are, a million years lost, and they don't exist. The things we worried about for months, a lifetime, not even born or thought of yet."

"Safety catches off, everyone!' ordered Travis. "You, first shot, Eckels. Second, Billings. Third, Kramer."

"I've hunted tiger, wild boar, buffalo, elephant, but now, this is *it*," said Eckels. "I'm shaking like a kid."

"Ah," said Travis.

Everyone stopped.

Travis raised his hand. "Ahead," he whispered. "In the mist. There he is. There's His Royal Majesty now."

The jungle was wide and full of twitterings, rustlings, murmurs, and sighs.

Suddenly it all ceased, as if someone had shut a door.

Silence.

A sound of thunder.

Out of the mist, one hundred yards away, came *Tyrannosaurus rex*.

"It," whispered Eckels. "It . . ."

"Sh!"

It came on great oiled, resilient, striding legs. It towered thirty feet above half of the trees, a great evil god, folding its delicate watchmaker's claws close to its oily, reptilian chest. Each lower leg was a piston, a thousand pounds of white bone, sunk in thick ropes of muscle, sheathed over in a gleam of pebbled skin like the mail of a terrible warrior. Each thigh was a ton of meat, ivory, and steel mesh. And from the great breathing cage of the upper body those two delicate arms dangled out front, arms with hands which might pick up and examine men like toys, while the snake neck coiled. And the head itself, a ton of sculptured stone, lifted easily upon the sky. Its mouth gaped, exposing a fence of teeth like daggers. Its eyes rolled, ostrich eggs, empty of all expression save hunger. It closed its mouth in a death grin. It ran, its pelvic bones crushing aside trees and bushes, its taloned feet clawing damp earth, leaving prints six inches deep wherever it settled its weight. It ran with a gliding ballet step, far too poised and balanced for its ten tons. It moved into a sunlit arena warily, its beautifully reptilian hands feeling the air.

"Why, why—" Eckels twitched his mouth. "It could reach up and grab the moon."

"Sh!" Travis jerked angrily. "He hasn't seen us yet."

"It can't be killed." Eckels pronounced this verdict quietly, as if there could be no argument. He had weighed the evidence and that was his considered opinion. The rifle in his hands seemed a cap gun. "We were fools to come. This is impossible."

"Shut up!' hissed Travis.

"Nightmare."

"Turn around," commanded Travis. "Walk quietly to the Machine. We'll remit one half your fee."

"I didn't realize it would be this *big*," said Eckels. "I miscalculated, that's all. And now I want out."

"It *sees* us!"

"There's the red paint on its chest!"

The Tyrant Lizard raised itself. Its armored flesh glittered like a thousand green coins. The coins, crusted with slime, steamed. In the slime, tiny insects wriggled, so that the entire body seemed to twitch and undulate, even while the monster itself did not move. It exhaled. The stink of raw flesh blew down the wilderness.

"Get me out of here," said Eckels. "It was never like this before. I was always sure I'd come through alive. I had good guides, good safaris and safety. This time, I figured wrong. I've met my match and admit it. This is too much for me to get hold of."

"Don't run," said Lesperance. "Turn around. Hide in the Machine."

"Yes," Eckels seemed to be numb. He looked at his feet as if trying to make them move. He gave a grunt of helplessness.

"Eckels!"

He took a few steps, blinking, shuffling.

"Not that way!"

The Monster, at the first motion, lunged forward with a terrible scream. It covered one hundred yards in six seconds. The rifles jerked up and blazed fire. A windstorm from the beast's mouth engulfed them in the stench of slime and old blood. The monster roared, teeth glittering with sun.

Eckels, not looking back, walking blindly to the edge of the Path, his gun limp in his arm, stepped off the Path and walked, not knowing it, in the jungle. His feet sank into green moss. His legs moved him, and he felt alone and remote from the events behind.

The rifles cracked again. Their sound was lost in shriek and lizard thunder. The great level of the reptile's tail swung up, lashed sideways. Trees exploded in clouds of leaf and branch. The Monster twitched its jeweler's hands down to fondle at the men, to twist them in half, to crush them like berries, to cram them into its teeth and its screaming throat. Its boulderstone eyes leveled with the men. They saw themselves mirrored. They fired at the metallic eyelids and blazing black irises.

Like a stone idol, like a mountain avalanche, *Tyrannosaurus* fell. Thundering, it clutched trees, pulled them with it. It wrenched and tore the metal Path. The men flung themselves back and away. The body hit, ten tons of cold flesh and stone. The guns fired. The Monster lashed its armored tail, twitched its snake jaws and lay still. A fount of blood spurted from its throat. Somewhere inside, a sac of fluid burst. Sickening gushes drenched the hunters. They stood, red and glistening.

The thunder faded.

The jungle was silent. After the avalanche, a green peace. After the nightmare, morning.

Billings and Kramer sat on the pathway and threw up. Travis and Lesperance stood with smoking rifles, cursing steadily.

In the Time Machine, on his face, Eckels lay shivering. He had found his way back to the Path, climbed into the Machine.

Travis came walking, glanced at Eckels, took cotton gauze from a metal box and returned to the others, who were sitting on the Path.

"Clean up."

They wiped the blood from their helmets. They began to curse too. The Monster lay, a hill of solid flesh. Within, you could hear the sighs and murmurs as the farthest chambers of it died, the organs malfunctioning, liquids running a final instant from pocket to sac to spleen, everything shutting off, closing up forever. It was like standing by a wrecked locomotive or a steam shovel at quitting time, all valves being released or levered tight. Bones cracked; the tonnage of its own flesh, off balance, dead weight, snapped the delicate forearms, caught underneath. The meat settled, quivering.

Another cracking sound. Overhead, a gigantic tree branch broke from its heavy mooring, fell. It crashed upon the dead beast with finality.

"There." Lesperance checked his watch. "Right on time. That's the giant tree that was scheduled to fall and kill this animal originally." He glanced at the two hunters. "You want the trophy picture?"

"What?"

"We can't take a trophy back to the Future. The body has to stay right where it would have died originally, so the insects, birds, and bacteria can get at it, as they were intended to. Everything in balance. The body stays. But we can take a picture of you standing near it."

The two men tried to think, but gave up, shaking their heads.

They let themselves be led along the metal Path. They sank wearily into the machine cushions. They gazed back at the ruined Monster, the stagnating mound, where already strange reptilian birds and golden insects were busy at the steaming armor.

A sound on the floor of the Time Machine stiffened them. Eckels sat there, shivering.

"I'm sorry," he said at last.

"Get up!" cried Travis.

Eckels got up.

"Go out on that Path alone," said Travis. He had his rifle pointed. "You're not coming back in the Machine. We're leaving you here!"

Lesperance seized Travis's arm. "Wait—"

"Stay out of this!" Travis shook his hand away. "This fool nearly killed us. But it isn't *that* so much, no. It's his *shoes*! Look at them! He ran off the Path. That *ruins* us! We'll forfeit! Thousands of dollars of insurance! We guaranteed no one leaves the Path. He left it. Oh, the fool! I'll have to report to the government. They might revoke our license to travel. Who knows *what* he's done to Time, to History!"

"Take it easy. All he did was kick up some dirt."

"How do we *know*?" cried Travis. "We don't know anything! It's all a mystery! Get out of here, Eckels!"

Eckels fumbled his shirt. "I'll pay anything. A hundred thousand dollars!"

Travis glared at Eckels's checkbook and spat. "Go out there. The Monster's next to the Path. Stick your arms up to your elbows in his mouth. Then you can

RAY BRADBURY

come back with us."

"That's unreasonable!"

"The Monster's dead, you idiot. The bullets! The bullets can't be left behind. They don't belong in the Past; they might change anything. Here's my knife. Dig them out!"

The jungle was alive again, full of the old tremorings and bird cries. Eckels turned slowly to regard the primeval garbage dump, that hill of nightmares and terror. After a long time, like a sleepwalker he shuffled out along the Path.

He returned, shuddering, five minutes later, his arms soaked and red to the elbow. He turned out his hands. Each held a number of steel bullets. Then he fell. He lay where he fell, not moving.

"You didn't have to make him do that," said Lesperance.

"Didn't I? It's too early to tell." Travis nudged the still body. "He'll live. Next time he won't go hunting game like this. Okay." He jerked his thumb wearily at Lesperance. "Switch on. Let's go home."

1492. 1776. 1812.

They cleaned their hands and faces. They changed their caking shirts and pants. Eckels was up and around again, not speaking. Travis glared at him for a full ten minutes.

"Don't look at me," cried Eckels. "I haven't done

anything."

"Who can tell?"

"Just ran off the Path, that's all, a little mud on my shoes—what do you want me to do, get down and pray?"

"We might need it. I'm warning you, Eckels, I might kill you yet. I've got my gun ready."

"I'm innocent. I've done nothing!"

1999. 2000. 2055.

The Machine stopped.

"Get out," said Travis.

The room was there as they had left it. But not the same as they had left it. The same man sat behind the same desk. But the same man did not quite sit behind the same desk.

Travis looked around swiftly. "Everything okay here?" he snapped.

"Fine. Welcome home!"

Travis did not relax. He seemed to be looking at the very atoms of the air itself, at the way the sun poured through the one high window.

"Okay, Eckels, get out. Don't ever come back."

Eckels could not move.

"You heard me," said Travis. "What're you *staring* at?"

Eckels stood smelling of the air, and there was a thing to the air, a chemical taint so subtle, so slight, that only a faint cry of his subliminal senses warned him it was there.

The colors, white, gray, blue, orange, in the wall, in the furniture, in the sky beyond the window, were . . . were . . . And there was a *feel*. His flesh twitched. His hands twitched. He stood drinking the oddness with the pores of his body. Somewhere, someone must have been screaming one of those whistles that only a dog can hear. His body screamed silence in return. Beyond this room, beyond this wall, beyond this man who was not quite the same man seated at this desk that was not quite the same desk . . . lay an entire world of streets and people. What sort of world it was now, there was no telling. He could feel them moving there, beyond the walls, almost, like so many chess pieces blown in a dry wind. . . .

But the immediate thing was the sign painted on the office wall, the same sign he had read earlier today on first entering.

Somehow, the sign had changed.

TYME SEFARI INC.

SEFARIS TU ANY YEER EN THE PAST.

YU NAIM THE ANIMALL.

WEE TAEK YU THAIR.

YU SHOOT ITT.

Eckels felt himself fall into the chair. He fumbled

crazily at the thick slime on his boots. He held up a clod of dirt, trembling. "No, it *can't* be. Not a *little* thing like that. No!"

Embedded in the mud, glistening green and gold and black, was a butterfly, very beautiful and very dead.

"Not a little thing like *that*! Not a butterfly!" cried Eckels.

It fell to the floor, an exquisite thing, a small thing that could upset balances and knock down a line of small dominoes and then big dominoes and then gigantic dominoes, all down the years across Time. Eckels's mind whirled. It *couldn't* change things. Killing one butterfly couldn't be *that* important! Could it?

His face was cold. His mouth trembled, asking: "Who—who won the presidential election yesterday?"

The man behind the desk laughed. "You joking? You know very well. Deutscher, of course! Who else? Not that fool weakling Keith. We got an iron man now, a man with guts!" The official stopped. "What's wrong?"

Eckels moaned. He dropped to his knees. He scrabbled at the golden butterfly with shaking fingers. "Can't we," he pleaded to the world, to himself, to the officials, to the Machine, "can't we take it *back,* can't we *make* it alive again? Can't we start over? Can't we—"

He did not move. Eyes shut, he waited, shivering. He heard Travis breathe loud in the room; he heard Travis shift his rifle, click the safety catch and raise the weapon.

There was a sound of thunder.

Ray Bradbury

Ray Bradbury was born in 1920 in Waukegan, Illinois. In 1934, the Bradbury family moved to Los Angeles, California, where young Ray graduated from Los Angeles High School in 1938. His formal education ended at that point, but Bradbury continued to educate himself—through reading at the library by night and working at his typewriter as time permitted by day. From 1938 to 1942, Bradbury sold newspapers on Los Angeles street corners, but after selling his first story, he gave up his job and began writing full-time. In 1945 his short story "The Big Black and White Game" was selected for *Best American Short Stories*, and in that same year he published *Dark Carnival*, his first short story collection.

His reputation as a leading science fiction writer was established with the publication of *The Martian Chronicles* in 1950. This famous vignette collection chronicles the attempts of Earthlings to colonize Mars. Bradbury released another best-seller in 1953. In *Fahrenheit 451*, Bradbury describes a future in which the written word is forbidden and all books are burned.

Bradbury has won numerous awards for his writing, including the Benjamin Franklin Award, the

Aviation-Space Writer's Association Award, the World Fantasy Award for lifetime achievement, and the Grand Master Award from the Science Fiction Writers of America. His animated film, *Icarus Montgolfier Wright*, was nominated for an Academy Award, and his teleplay of *The Halloween Tree* won an Emmy. Perhaps the most unique honor Bradbury has received for his writing was when an Apollo astronaut named a crater on the moon "Dandelion Crater" after Bradbury's novel, *Dandelion Wine*.

Even though he's been called the greatest science fiction writer in the world, Bradbury thinks of himself as an "idea writer." "My stories have led me through my life," he once said. "They shout, I follow. They run up and bite me on the leg—I respond by writing down everything that goes on during the bite. When I finish, the idea lets go, and runs off."

I. THE STORY LINE
A. Digging for Facts

1. The group of hunters is traveling back through time to hunt a (a) pterodactyl; (b) Tyrannosaurus rex; (c) giant mammoth.

2. Time Safari has provided a path for the hunters (a) to keep them from being harmed by creatures of the prehistoric jungle; (b) as a precaution against changing the future; (c) so that they can easily move in the dense jungle.

3. According to Travis, the most extreme result of killing a mouse could be killing a (a) billion mice; (b) lion; (c) race of people.

4. The hunters are allowed to shoot only animals that (a) are marked with red paint; (b) are a threat to their safety; (c) do not have young.

5. Before each safari, Lesperance goes back in time to (a) discover how each expedition turns out; (b) make sure the path has not been damaged; (c) look for animals that will die soon.

6. According to Lesperance, a man meeting himself in time travel would be a/an (a) paradox; (b) fluke; (c) oxymoron.

7. When the creature shows up, Eckels (a) fires before Travis gives the signal; (b) faints; (c) proves himself to be a coward.

8. To punish Eckels for his actions, Travis orders him to (a) pay a fine of $5,000; (b) remove the bullets from the creature's body; (c) help the other men clean up.

9. One of the changes the group discovers upon returning to the year 2055 has to do with the (a) presidential election; (b) pronunciation of certain words; (c) value assigned to money.

10. When Eckels checks the bottom of his shoe, he finds that he has crushed a (a) mouse; (b) butterfly; (c) dinosaur egg.

B. Probing for Theme

A *theme* is a central message of a piece of literature. Read the thematic statements below. Which one best applies to "A Sound of Thunder"? Be prepared to support your opinion.

1. Humans should not interfere with the natural order of things.

2. Because all life is interrelated, a seemingly insignificant event can have huge consequences.

3. Technology has the potential to destroy the human race.

II. IN SEARCH OF MEANING

1. What is the difference between the two presidential candidates, Keith and Deutscher? Why might Bradbury have chosen "Deutscher" as the name for one of the candidates?

2. Why does the man at the travel agency purposely try to scare Eckels out of going on the safari? Why do you think Eckels couldn't be scared off by the man but is not able to go through with the hunt once it begins?

3. What is Travis's theory about having contact with any aspect of the prehistoric jungle?

4. According to Lesperance, why can't a person meet him- or herself during time travel?

5. Why doesn't Eckels do as Travis tells him and go back into the machine once the hunt begins?

6. Why do Billings and Kramer refuse the trophy picture?

7. Travis's first reaction to what Eckels has done is to order him to stay behind in the jungle. Why would it not be feasible for Travis to leave Eckels behind?

8. Was Eckels's punishment for leaving the path fair? Why or why not?

9. In what ways has the world changed since the hunters left for their safari? In particular, how has the man behind the desk changed? What might this change indicate about the world the hunters have returned to?

10. What do you think happens at the end of the story?

III. DEVELOPING WORD POWER

Exercise A

Each of the following words appears in a sentence taken directly from the text. Read the sentence, and then select the correct meaning from the four choices.

1. merest

   "A touch of a hand might do it, the *merest* touch of a hand."

   a. tender   c. comforting

   b. slightest   d. shocking

2. annihilate

   "With a stamp of your foot, you *annihilate* first one, then a dozen, then a thousand, a million, a billion possible mice."

   a. wipe out   c. affect

   b. terrify   d. bury

3. expendable

   "And the caveman, please note, is not just any *expendable* man, no!"

   a. reasonable   c. important

b. typical   d. replaceable

4. waxes

"Perhaps Europe is forever a dark forest, and only Asia *waxes* healthy and teeming."

a. seems   c. continues

b. returns   d. grows

5. infinitesimally

"Crushing certain plants could add up *infinitesimally*."

a. in a small way   c. in a terrifying way

b. in a huge way   d. in an unlimited way

6. subtle

"Maybe Time can't be changed by us. Or maybe it can be changed only in little, *subtle* ways."

a. harmful   c. not obvious

b. apparent   d. unimportant

7. paradox

"That'd be a *paradox*," said [Lesperance]. 'Time doesn't permit that sort of mess—a man meeting himself."

a. mystery   c. disaster

    b. disadvantage   d. contradiction

8. resilient

"It came on great oiled, *resilient*, striding legs."

    a. flexible   c. gigantic

    b. long   d. powerful

9. sheathed

"Each lower leg was a piston, a thousand pounds of white bone, sunk in thick ropes of muscle, *sheathed* over in a gleam of pebbled skin like the mail of a terrible warrior."

    a. glossed   c. covered

    b. stretched   d. anchored

10. undulate

"In the slime, tiny insects wriggled, so that the entire body seemed to twitch and *undulate*, even while the monster itself did not move."

    a. jerk   c. ripple

    b. bend   d. swerve

Exercise B

Below is a list of vocabulary words (or a form of each) from the story. Choose the word that best completes the sentences that follow the list.

a. annihilation   f. resilient

b. expendable   g. sheath

c. infinitesimally   h. subtle

d. merest   i. undulating

e. paradox   j. wax

1. Josh's parents bought him a/an __?__ camera for summer camp so that he wouldn't have to take their expensive one.

2. To avoid accidental injury, the Scouts were ordered to __?__ their knives when they weren't using them.

3. The insecure toddler cried at the __?__ indication that her mother might be going out.

4. Some considered it a/an __?__ that the girls won the state championship but lost earlier in the year to a small, inexperienced team.

5. Never one to display his feelings, the father let his daughter know he loved her in __?__ ways.

6. "Children are very __?__," the psychologist explained. "They are usually able to recover quickly from a bad experience."

7. The boat sailed smoothly over the gently __?__ water.

8. In order to prevent __?__ of a species, hunting laws limit the number of kills a hunter can make.

9. "Within a few days the new moon will __?__ to its full phase," Professor Bloomer told his astronomy students.

10. The votes surprised everyone by adding up __?__, causing one candidate to win by a very small margin.

IV. IMPROVING WRITING SKILLS

Exercise A

Choose one of the following activities.

1. Bradbury is considered a master of descriptive language. Look closely at his description of the Tyrannosaurus rex on page 14. What action verbs bring the animal to life for the reader? What adjectives allow the reader to "see" the monster? Imitating Bradbury's style, write your own description of a terrifying situation or creature.

2. Science fiction writers have always been fascinated by time travel. What is the lure of time travel? What would be the benefits to being able to go back in time? What might be the drawbacks? Write a paper that presents your views on this subject. Begin with a statement that explains the lure of time travel. Then use either the block method or the point-by-point method to describe the benefits and drawbacks. If you choose to use the block method, you will present a block of ideas about the benefits and then a block of ideas about the drawbacks. If you decide to use the point-by-point method, you will alternate repetitively between benefits and drawbacks.

Exercise B

Ray Bradbury feared that humans would destroy themselves through technology. In this story he conveys that fear by showing the kind of disaster that could result from time travel. Do you think Bradbury is justified in his fear? Is it unavoidable that advancements in technology will eventually destroy the human race? Or do you think humans are wise and cautious enough to avoid such a fate?

Write a persuasive essay in which you try to convince your audience to agree with your opinion. Begin with a statement that indicates your opinion on Bradbury's theory. Then support your opinion with examples, facts, statistics, etc. End your essay by rephrasing your opinion statement and then including a strong statement or thought-provoking idea that reinforces your opinion while making your audience remember your essay.

V. THINGS TO WRITE OR TALK ABOUT

1. Do you think time travel might someday be possible? If not, why not? If so, do you think it should be pursued? Explain.

2. The idea that stepping on a butterfly can change the course of history is based on *chaos theory*. *Chaos theory* contends that complex and unpredictable results can occur from seemingly insignificant incidents. How might chaos theory explain ecological changes today (for example, the extinction of certain animals)? If chaos theory holds true, what human activities might have complex and unpredictable results?

3. Do you think Eckels was really a coward or was he simply reacting the way most people would react in the circumstances? Provide details from the story to support your opinion.

4. *Foreshadowing* is the use of clues that hint at what is going to happen later in a story. What clues does Bradbury drop that indicate what will happen during the hunt? What things might be changed upon the hunters' return to 2055? How the story will end? Why do you think a writer would choose to use foreshadowing?

5. What are the two sounds of thunder in the story? What might the sound of thunder symbolize in this story?

ANSWER KEY

I. THE STORY LINE
A. Digging for Facts

1. b	6. a
2. b	7. c
3. c	8. b
4. a	9. a
5. c	10. b

B. Probing for Theme

Students may elect to support any of the three choices. The suggested answer is *Because all life is interrelated, a seemingly insignificant event can have huge consequences.* When Eckels wanders off the path, he comes into physical contact with the prehistoric jungle. In doing so, he crushes a butterfly. That seemingly insignificant incident changes the course of history by setting off a chain of events that results in the kind of world the men find when they return from their safari. Had Eckels not interfered with the butterfly's lifespan, a different chain of events would have occurred—the chain that led to the kind of world the hunters had originally left.

III. DEVELOPING WORD POWER

Exercise A

1. merest

   b. slightest

2. annihilate

   a. wipe out

3. expendable

   d. replaceable

4. waxes

   d. grows

5. infinitesimally

   a. in a small way

6. subtle

   c. not obvious

7. paradox

   d. contradiction